MARY STOLZ
DEPUTY SHEP

illustrated by Pamela Johnson

HarperCollins_Publishers_

1   2   3   4   5   6   7   8   9   10
First Edition

Library of Congress Cataloging-in-Publication Data

Stolz, Mary, date
   Deputy Shep / by Mary Stolz ; illustrated by Pamela Johnson.
      p.   cm.
   Summary: Deputy Jack Shep, the laziest police dog to ever wear a badge,
is called upon to investigate a wave of burglaries in the sleepy village of
Canoville.
   ISBN 0-06-026039-4.—ISBN 0-06-026040-8 (lib.bdg.)
   [1. Dogs—Fiction.   2. Mystery and detective stories.]
I. Johnson, Pamela, ill.   II. Title.
PZ7.S875854De 1991   90-38664
[Fic]—dc20   CIP
                                                                   AC

This book
is dedicated, with great affection,
to Helen Swift and Michael Lunskis,
exemplars of a wonderful breed:
The Librarian.

1

BY FIVE THIRTY in the evening, sheriff's deputy Jack Shep had finished breakfast. He patted his whiskers with a linen napkin, took his dishes to the sink, washed them, and left them on the drainboard to dry. He checked to be sure that his kitchen was tidy, that the clock did not need winding, and that his cat, Beanblossom, had food and water.

"*Ciao*, Beanblossom," he said. "See you in the morning."

"*Miao*," said the cat.

Taking his dinner pail, Shep stepped out

on the porch and drew a deep breath of the fragrant summer dusk. With a few minutes left before he need start for the station house, he went into his garden to do battle with weeds.

He was so busy that he failed to hear the six-o'clock church bells. Doctor Dane, going by in his old two-wheeled rig, stopped and said, "Evening, Shep. Do you realize it's gone six?"

"Oh, boy!" Shep exclaimed, scrambling to his feet. "Thanks, Doc. I'd forget my head if it wasn't—"

"Tied on," said Doctor Dane. He clucked to his little cart mare, Fiddlesticks, and was off in puffs of dust.

There was only one doctor in the village of Canoville, and he was a lot busier than its two police officers, of which Jack Shep was one. There was little crime in the village, but of sickness and broken bones there was no end. And births, of course. And deaths. And only Doctor Dane to cure, to comfort, to console. No wonder he was always in a hurry and sometimes a bit snappish.

Shep dusted earth from the knees of his uniform, mounted his bicycle, and pedaled slowly toward the station house.

Sheriff Phil English sat behind his desk reading the police dog's manual. "You're late again, Deputy," he barked. "And your uniform is dirty."

"Sorry, Phil." Shep put his dinner pail on a shelf and glanced at the clock. "I'll add fifteen minutes onto the end of my tour."

Sheriff English pawed the air. "Tonight you will spend your whole twelve hours on point duty. That's an order."

"Point duty doing what? Where?"

"You will stand at the corner of Main and Church and direct traffic."

"Traffic? If two bicycles and a cat go by from now till morning, it'd be a wonder."

"You will make sure the bicycles don't collide and that the cat doesn't disturb the peace. Darn cats are a bunch of rowdies."

"My cat, Beanblossom—"

"Is a domestic pet," the sheriff interrupted. "Not an alley ruffian. One of these days I'll run the lot of them out of town."

"You tell 'em, Phil."

4

The sheriff had as much chance of getting cats to behave as he had of getting his own pups to. As for running them out of town, he might as well say he'd run the river out of town. Cats and rivers go their own way.

"Now, listen up, Deputy," the sheriff was going on. "*I* am your superior officer, and I will not tolerate familiarity. You will address me as Sheriff. Or Sir. *Chief* would be nice."

"Are you forgetting—Sheriff, Sir—that tomorrow is the first of July?"

The sheriff moved his inkwell an inch to the right, a half inch to the left. He straightened the desk blotter. He smoothed his whiskers. Snarling slightly, he said, "I take your point, Deputy."

"And take me off point duty?" said Jack Shep. He chuckled happily.

"One thing not necessary in a police dog, Deputy, is a sense of humor. Not that you're funny," Phil English said irritably.

They were silent for a while. The sheriff was in no hurry to go home, as his pups were noisy and knew even less about discipline than Jack Shep or the cats. And the deputy was hoping that nothing had happened during the day that would require his attention tonight. Jack Shep liked an unblotted police blotter and a quiet tour of duty that left him undisturbed in the station house, except for town rounds twice nightly.

Now he looked around the small room. It was neat and clean. There was a cast-iron stove in one corner, cold now in summer, with a pot of bright geraniums on the lid. A door to an inner room had "Captain" written on it in gold lettering. It was used for a lockup when they had somebody to lock up. There was no captain, never had been or would be. Jack Shep and Phil English were the town's police force, and

"Sheriff" was as high up the constabulary ladder as they'd go. The local banker and mayor and head of the Board of Aldermen, Enoch Peke IV, said Canoville had no call to pay for a captain of police.

Shep was sorry that tomorrow would begin his time to be sheriff and Phil's to be deputy. They took turns at it, six months each. Phil, who liked to give orders, was better at being top officer than was Jack, who did not like to.

Now Shep said warily, "Anything on the blotter, Chief?"

Pleased by that "Chief," Phil said in a friendlier tone, "We've got another robbery. I mean burglary."

Deputy Shep sighed. There went his quiet evening, probably. "What's the difference?" he asked.

"Read your manual, Deputy. You're robbed if you're on the premises, and burgled if you are not on them."

"I meant what's the difference what we call it. It still comes out to we have to investigate. Not that it's done any good so far."

"Jack Shep—you have to be the laziest police dog who ever wore a badge! It's the first chance we've had to investigate a crime since we caught that fox trespassing—"

"We never proved he was—" Shep began, but was interrupted again.

"It isn't as if we had enough—I mean, a lot—of crime to look into," the sheriff said fretfully. "We have to grab what comes our way."

"Who got burgled?"

"The Enoch Pekes."

"Oh boy. And where were they when the crime took place?"

"Taking a walk, they say."

"Don't you believe them?"

"Why shouldn't I believe them?"

"Then why do you say 'they say'?"

"Because it's what they said."

Officer Shep scratched his ear. "If you say 'they say,'" he began, "that sounds as if you think they're just saying it."

"They *were* just saying it. What can you say about taking a walk except to say that you were taking it?"

Deputy Shep gave up. "What got stolen?"

"Mrs. Peke's valuable ruby dog collar."

"Ruby?"

"That's what they say."

"Do you think they're just saying that, too?"

"How do I know? While they were taking a walk a burglar got in and took Mrs. Peke's ruby collar. That's what Enoch told me. He came in just before you got here, shouting and waving his tail, telling me to call him *Mister* Peke. I have as good a family tree as he has, maybe better. I'll Mister him when he Sirs me."

9

"Why wasn't Mrs. Peke wearing this valuable ruby collar?" Shep asked, relieved to have missed Enoch Peke IV's visit to the station house.

"Enoch says she doesn't wear valuables when she's just taking a walk. Go round right away and get their statements."

"Why didn't you do that?" Shep exclaimed. Now he'd have to face Enoch after all, and not only him, but also Mrs. Peke. Rats!

"No time," said Sheriff English, with a pleased expression.

"You said I was to go on point duty, Phil. I mean Sir. I mean Chief—"

"Forget about point duty. You go see his nibs. Mind you don't get his dander up, Shep. Keep in mind that he's the mayor and the town banker, and head of the Board of Aldermen, and you—what shall I say? Well, put it this way. *You* are a long way from being any of those. At the same time, make sure you insist that the full respect due our constabulary position is observed. I demand respect."

"Some things can't be demanded," Shep mumbled.

"What was that, Deputy? What did you mutter there?"

"I said—the perp must be remanded."

"We have to catch him first," the sheriff growled. He donned his cap and tramped out of the station.

11

‖

WHEN THE SHERIFF had gone, Deputy Shep spent a few minutes looking busy. Phil had a trick of suddenly reappearing.

"Forgot my dinner pail," he'd say, having left it behind on purpose.

Thinks he'll find me yawning behind the desk, thought Shep. He walked to the file cabinets, pulled out a drawer, and studied the burglary reports, all written by the sheriff. Shep had never bothered to read them before.

"Well, looky here," he muttered aloud. "Four burglaries. All perpetrated in daylight. Hmmm, hum, hmmm. What can it mean?" A burglar afraid of the dark? Maybe a burglar who liked to sleep nights. Most dogs did. That's why Shep himself liked night duty. He liked pounding his beat when other dogs were pounding the pillow.

Mrs. Whippet had reported her cameo brooch missing. *(Hrlm.,v.val)* read Phil English's entry. Heirloom, very valuable. There was a similar notation on the report of Mrs. Aire-Setter's silver coffee spoon. Major Ridgeback, K-9 Corps (Ret.), was missing a war medal, entered by the sheriff as having *(Mch snt.val)*. Much sentimental value. And today Phil had written on the Peke sheet *(Ext.Val.Encr/rubies)*. Extremely valuable, encrusted with rubies.

Jack Shep nodded to himself. He'd seen that old cameo of Mrs. Whippet's, and of course the Major was never without the war medal on his lapel. What would be the worth of an heirloom silver spoon, or of a dog collar encrusted with rubies?

Well, his not to question the value of these valuables. His to investigate what had happened to them, if he could figure where to begin. According to Phil's reports, there was a peculiar, not to say cuckoo, aspect to these burglaries. In every case, one valuable object had been taken and a button of no value left behind.

A button. Every time. What was to be made of that?

Deciding he could make nothing of it, Shep yawned and returned the folder to the file drawer. Enough time had passed so that he could be sure Phil wouldn't suddenly pop back, but even so he couldn't relax. There was that statement to take from the Enoch Pekes, and the sooner he got at it, the sooner he'd get it behind him. He put on his cap, made sure he had his flashlight, notebook, and pencil, and started off reluctantly.

What he wished to do, and usually did do, for the first couple of hours of his duty tour, was to lean back in the desk chair and consult seed and garden catalogs. Shep's gardens were his main interest. Flowers in the front yard, vegetables in the back. After going through his catalogs for an hour or so, he would set out for the night's first round of village streets and alleys. Now and then he was obliged to quiet a fence crowd of howling cats. From time to time, he made a pretense of apprehending a marauding raccoon, a vagrant armadillo, once a suspicious-looking fox. Not since joining the force had Shep made an arrest.

His first tour finished, he would then return to the station house, water the geranium, open his dinner pail, spread a large napkin on the desk, tuck another under his chin, and dine. A nap on a bench under the window, and he'd be ready for his second inspection of the sleeping town.

Later, back at the desk, he'd pull the blotter toward him and write: *A.q. Nthng to rpt.* All quiet. Nothing to report.

Now these burglaries had altered his pattern. Trotting across the green to Enoch Peke's house, Shep thought that for once he was having to behave like the police dog he was supposed to be, rather than the lazy dog he actually was.

"You should be ashamed," he said to himself. But he wasn't.

Enoch Peke IV met him at the door. "We've been waiting for you, Deputy. Took your time, didn't you? Don't bother to explain," he said to Shep, who hadn't planned to. "Come in, come in."

"Much obliged." Shep stepped over the sill and greeted Enoch's young son, who

16

paused halfway up the stairs to grin over his shoulder. "Hi, Bert. How's tricks?"

"Got at least one I could tell you about," Bert began, but was interrupted by his father.

"To your room, Ethelbert," Enoch Peke said sharply. "This minute. And you, officer, step in here."

Bossy, thought Shep. Used to having his way.

A large cat was lying underneath a birdcage that was shrouded for the night. Mrs. Peke was lying on the sofa, eyes rolled back.

"Is she sick?" the deputy inquired. "I could come back later."

"Only swooning. Been doing it off and on all day, ever since we discovered the ruby dog collar missing."

Officer Shep got out his notebook and wrote, *Vic. swning o. & o.* Victim swooning off and on.

"She's been doing that all day?" he asked.

"I just said so. Don't like having to repeat."

"Have you called Doctor Dane?"

"Don't want him. He's too big. Last time he was here the floor sagged."

Mrs. Peke sat up. "Why can't we have two doctors in town, that's all I have to say. Oh, before we moved here, we had such a *fine* physician. Doctor Scotti. So reassuring, and a dog of a reasonable *size*. A wirehair. We need two doctors in this town more than we need two policemen, that's all I have to say."

Deputy Shep didn't think it was all she had to say. "What can you tell me about this affair?"

Mr. and Mrs. Peke burst into speech together.

"We weren't gone more than half an hour—"

"We were just taking a short walk—"

"And when we got back, the collar was *gone*—"

"If the police were on the job—"

"Where was this collar, while you were taking this walk?" Shep interrupted.

"On the mantel," said Mr. Peke. "Mrs. Peke wore it last night when we attended a lodge dinner. Got home quite late. Didn't want to take it to the vault at that hour. After all, we expect better of our police force than to permit citizens of our standing to be robbed—"

"Burgled," Shep said to himself, and aloud, "You say this was a ruby dog collar?"

Enoch Peke's chest swelled. "We don't *say* it was, we *tell* you it was. A collar studded with rubies. What are you suggesting, Deputy Shep?"

"I wasn't sugges—"

"See here, Deputy Shep," Mr. Peke interrupted. "Unless you apologize and withdraw your suggestion that the collar is not studded with rubies, I may have to take action."

"I don't mind apologizing, Enoch. I mean, Mayor Peke, Sir. Anyway, it wasn't a suggestion. Only I can't understand why you'd leave such a valuable collar lying around. I mean, why wasn't Mrs. Peke wearing it?"

"My wife does *not* wear jewels in the daytime." His tone made clear that anyone but a common police dog would know that the wearing of rubies by daylight was vulgar.

"Well then." Shep closed his notebook. "I guess we've covered everything."

"What are you going to do about recovering our property, Deputy Shep? I fail to see that you've covered that."

"Have to see how things shape up, don't I? I won't get anywhere standing around here." He hadn't been asked to sit down the whole time, and was doing a little resenting of his own. Manners were manners. Even if Peke here was a banker and an alderman and the mayor, and himself a lowly member of the constabulary, manners were manners. "I'll be getting along."

"I expect to hear from you soon, Deputy. As in immediately."

Shep started off, turned back. "By the way, did you find a button on the mantel?"

"Button?" said the banker. "No, we didn't find any—"

"We did too!" Mrs. Peke shrieked, sitting up. "There was a button, right *there* where my beautiful collar had been."

"What kind of a button?" Shep asked.

"No *kind* of button. A button you'd find on any cheap sweater. Nothing *I* would think of wearing."

"Any particular color?"

"I tell you, it was just a button. A tarnished brass button."

Vlgr but'n lft on mnt'l, Deputy Shep noted. Vulgar button left on mantel. "May I see it?"

"See it? You don't think I kept it? It's in the trash."

At this, Shep put a finger to his cap and went off with a low contented growl.

GLANCING IN the Pekes' living-room window, to be sure they were still there, Deputy Shep went around to the back of the house and took the lid off the trash barrel.

"Aha!" he muttered. "What do you know."

Lying atop crumpled papers was a brass button, without doubt the button in question. It was plainly too inelegant for Mrs. Peke.

It was a medium-sized brass button, not very tarnished, indeed still glinting with a bit of the old shine. There was an anchor embossed on it, but Shep did not conclude a sea-going perp. Any small dog in town

might have lost it from his sailor suit. Pocketing the button, Shep mounted his bicycle and pedaled slowly along, stopping now and then to study a neighbor's garden.

At the firehouse, Chief Dal was currying his enormous draft horse, Henry. The town's gleaming red fire wagon stood with its shafts on the ground.

"Greetings, Shep," said the chief. "Early, aren't you?"

"I had to go by Enoch Peke's and get a statement."

"About the collar crammed with rubies?"

"Where did you hear about it?"

"Things get around. You got any leads?"

"Of course not."

Chief Dal backed Henry into his stall, filled the bin with oats and the trough with fresh water, and came out to sit beside Shep. He lit his pipe and blew smoke that smelled like a chocolate bar.

They remained comfortably silent for a while, listening to the sleepy songs of birds settling for the night, to the crisp tuning up of insects in the grass, to the hollow clopping and loud munching going on behind them—Henry at supper.

Fred Dober, the lamplighter, came by. He lifted a long pole to the streetlamp in front of the station. Hooking a small chain under the globe, he pulled, and the mantle lit up with a soft glow.

" 'Evening, Fred," said the chief.

" 'Evening," said the lamplighter, and trudged on without a backward glance.

In a short while the beautiful Madame Colette drove by in her little black cabriolet. It had Chinese-red wheels, a red-velvet bench, a black canopy with red fringe that swayed as her high-stepping horse trotted past. The lovely French poodle waved her little driving whip at the two outside the firehouse.

"Bon soir, bon soir, mes amis!" she called melodiously.

Chief Dal sighed. "The prettiest sight this town has to offer, wouldn't you say, Shep?"

"It certainly is a neat little cab," Shep said.

"I was *referring*, Jack, to Madame Colette. A vision of loveliness. *Floats* by like a swan. Her wheels don't even raise dust. You lack the romantic strain."

"Probably," said Shep.

Another silence, interrupted by church bells informing the village of the hour of eight.

"Any fires today?" Shep inquired.

"Nope."

"When was the last one?"

"Can't remember."

"Phil thinks this town's too quiet," said Shep. "He wants something to *happen*. He wants exciting reports to read when he comes on duty."

"He's got a robbery. That should please him."

"Burglary."

"Huh?"

"Robbery is when—" Deputy Shep began, then waved a paw. "Doesn't matter. But you're right—it'll keep him busy searching for clues and stuff." He wondered if those buttons were a clue.

"See here, Chief," he said, "I've got this problem."

"Do my best to help, Shep."

"Well . . . it's like this. I was poking around in the files, trying to look busy in case Phil sneaked back on me, and I read about these burglaries. The thing is— every time something got taken, something got left in its place."

"A bartering burglar, eh? What does he leave behind?"

"Buttons."

"What kind of buttons?"

"No-account buttons, lacking in refinement. Mrs. Peke sniffs at the one that was left on her mantel."

"She sniffs a lot, doesn't she?"

"The thing is," Shep went on, "I can't decide whether to include in my report the part about the button on the Pekes' mantel. And that I went around the house and poked in their trash and there it was. The sheriff isn't going to like it. I mean that *I* found the button instead of him. He'll think I'm showing off."

"That so?" the chief said absently. He was gazing down the road in the direction the lovely poodle had taken in her cabriolet, leaving but the gentlest stir of dust in her wake.

IV

NEAR THE EDGE of town, Shep encountered
Doctor Dane's rig coming toward him. The
doctor reined in Fiddlesticks, who dropped
her head, while Doc, looming like a statue
in the park, leaned his big jaw on his big
paw.

"You look beat, Doc," Shep said.

"I am. We need two doctors in this
town."

"That's what Mrs. Peke says. She says
we need two doctors more than we need
two policemen."

"I don't know about that, Shep. You and

what's-his-name manage to keep the peace." He closed his eyes briefly. "Why were you hearing what Mrs. Peke thinks? Have they done something felonious?" he asked, perking up.

"It got done to them. Her ruby dog collar was burgled."

"Ruby, eh? Well, well."

"She's been swooning off and on all day from shock."

"Hope they don't call me in."

"Not much chance of that, Doc."

Doctor Dane smiled. He lifted the reins, let them fall, and said, "You going anywhere near Pete Bassett's place tonight?"

"Well, it's only a little off my round."

"Do me a favor, will you?"

"Sure thing, Doc."

"Stop by and see how he is. I just delivered the Missus of a litter of seven."

"How's Pete taking it?"

"How would you expect? Dithering and

whimpering, getting in the way, puffing and panting, tongue practically on the floor. Of course, these are his first seven children, so he's excited. He asked me to come by again later and I don't want to. I'm tired. Fiddlesticks here is tired."

"You get on home to bed. I'll stop and talk to Pete and admire the litter ones. I mean, I guess *she's* okay—Bridget Bassett—or you wouldn't—"

"Of course I wouldn't. She's fine, just fine. Well—I'll be seeing you, Deputy Shep. By the way, aren't you due to be sheriff one of these days?"

Jack Shep nodded without pleasure. "Tomorrow. I keep telling Phil I'd rather not, and he keeps saying 'regulations.' "

The doctor looked amused. "I'll bet he does. Just the same, you always make a good sheriff." He tapped the reins on the little horse's back. "Up, Fiddlesticks," he said gently. "We'll go home now. 'Night,

Shep. Thanks for helping out. You'll let me know if I'm needed—"

Deputy Shep watched their slow progress for a minute or two, then pedaled along the dusty road in the other direction.

He was now alongside the property of one of the richest dogs in town, the Widow Colly. Jack thought how having lots of money seemed to affect dogs in different ways. Mavis Peke sniffed and sneered. Madame Colette was laughing and friendly. But the Widow Colly expected *deference*. And she got it. Not from everyone, but she got it a lot from some.

Banker-Mayor-Alderman Peke ran around the widow in circles, his tongue hanging out. For her, Sheriff English swept off his cap and just kept from dropping to all fours. Citizens of the town went down before her like wheat in the wind, as if she were a species apart, not just another dog like themselves. She was, of course, very much a purebred—descended from a long line of border collies. Still, she was not the only thoroughbred in town.

Enoch Peke, if you could believe him, had a family tree with roots that twisted back to ancient Chinese dynasties. Phil English had as fine a line of bulldogs behind him as a cop could shake a nightstick at. Madame Colette was from one of the first families of Quebec. And Doctor Dane! The noblest, best-bred of them all.

So, said Jack to himself, it must be money that makes the widow strut like that.

Laying his bicycle down, he sat on a grassy bank leading to a duck pond that rippled softly in the evening breeze. Weeds and long grasses stirred gently at the water's edge. Swallows swooped to drink, skimming above the wavelets. Somewhere in the reeds, or hidden in clusters of water lilies, bullfrogs chorused.

Jack sighed with contentment.

Beyond the pond was Widow Colly's farm. The farmhouse was low and large, with blue-striped awnings at the windows, rattan rockers on the porch, and gardens surrounded by the richest, greenest grass imaginable.

On a rise beyond the house was a wind-mill, arms turning idly. Cows moved slowly in the meadow. The clink of their wooden bells, the creak of the windmill sails, the music of crickets and birds and bullfrogs, mingled to make Deputy Shep's eyelids heavy. He yawned, stretched, dropped into a light sleep in which he could hear the birds, the frogs, the windmill turning, the crickets and cowbells—the music of dreams . . .

"Hey you, Jack Shep! Wake up! I *said* wake up!"

"Huh?" Shep grunted. He tried to turn

over and resume his nap, was shaken by a rough paw. Forcing his eyes open, he found Junior Colly, the widow's son, standing over him, holding a snaffle bit.

"What's up, Junior?" he asked thickly.

"What's up is my mother's best mare has disappeared, while the town cop snores in the grass."

"I wasn't asleep. I was resting my eyes."

"Resting your eyes, my eye. Mother says you're to get on the stick and find her mare. Soon. As in right away."

Deputy Shep got to his feet, yawning, and pulled out his notebook. "What's she look like?"

"Small bay mare, two years old, name is Fancy That."

B. mare. Fncy Tht. Msng . . . Bay mare. Fancy That. Missing.

"How long's she been gone?" he asked, trying to swallow another yawn.

"Doggone it," Junior yelped. "Where's

Sheriff English? At least he stays awake when he's on duty."

"Now, now, Junior. Keep your collar on. You don't want to wake Phil. When he's off duty, he's off. Any idea of the mare's whereabouts?"

"If I did I wouldn't be talking to you, would I?"

Jack Shep frowned, scratched his ear. "I asked how long she's been gone."

"How should I know? Mother rode her up-pasture late this afternoon, then stabled her. After that we took a dip in the pool, and then had supper. So it could've been any time after Mother got back."

"Hmm. So you don't know—" Observing that Junior's lips were curling back, and knowing Junior operated on a short fuse, Shep closed his notebook, nodded, and said briskly, "I'll get right on it."

"See that you do."

Shep bristled. He had an even temper,

but it could be aroused. For a moment they stalked stiff-legged around each other, growling softly. Then Shep said, "Truce, Junior. If we get scrapping, I'll be in trouble with the sheriff and you'll be in trouble with your mother." Of the two, he'd take Sheriff English any day, and so, he suspected, would Junior.

"Here," said young Colly, thrusting the snaffle bit at Shep. "Take this. In case you get lucky and find her."

Shep didn't bother to be insulted. "Aren't you going to look for her yourself?" he asked.

"I'll pick up a snaffle in the stable. You just get started on your job—" Junior paused at a narrow glance from the police dog. "I mean, you'll want to get started, won't you, *Officer* Shep? Try the roads. I'll go across the fields."

Shep climbed the bank and mounted his

bicycle, trying to think where he'd go if he were a runaway horse.

If he had his way—and he saw no reason why the mare should not have hers unless she'd been abducted—he'd head for the hills. But Junior, who'd inherited his mother's commanding ways, had said try the roads.

Nothing but trouble came of bucking the mucky-mucks. He yawned again, switched on his bicycle lamp, and set off to try the roads.

Trouble was absolutely Deputy Shep's last choice in life.

WONDERING WHERE to start looking for a wayward mare in the gathering dusk, Deputy Shep leaned over his handlebars and pedaled furiously. Vigor might produce results.

If Fancy That had merely taken a fancy to wander off for a while, no doubt she'd return to her stable, her oats, her rubdown, when she'd had her run.

On the other hand, she could be, at this moment, in a horse van miles away, kidnapped by horse thieves whom they'd never catch up with.

"And what could I do about that?" Shep asked himself, pumping along with his tongue hanging out.

Doggone it, he growled to himself. A nice easy evening, and now this. Why couldn't it happen on Phil's watch? Even with nothing to do about it, the sheriff would've worked up the sense of duty he so enjoyed.

Am I really cut out for public service? Shep asked himself, slowing down. That is the question. Maybe I should hire out as a gardener. Ask Mrs. Colly if she could use another paw in her greenhouses, among her vegetables or border gardens?

He could hear himself . . .

"Mrs. Colly, ma'am, I am a dog with a green claw, and I want a job in your garden!"

Working for the widow, he'd have to wear a hat to doff. He'd be obliged to tuck in his tail at her approach.

None of that for him! He'd stay with the job he had and his own small garden.

Passing a side road, he braked, turned, wobbled down a rutty path. The Bassetts lived at the end of the lane here, and he'd promised Doc Dane to look in on them. That was something he *could* do.

Pete Bassett, a good-natured fellow with ears like shawls, was a dog who tried hard to keep his house and grounds in order, but everything seemed always to get ahead of him. He never seemed to get a job actually finished. Ants invaded his basement while he was on the roof replacing shingles. Coming down from the roof because he hadn't carried up enough shingles, he was apt to swing the ladder around and break a window. Repairing the window, he'd cut his paw. Trying to bandage it, he'd knock dishes to the floor and slice his other paw picking up the pieces. Meanwhile rain would drip through the unshingled part of the roof and ants make headway in the cellar.

So it went.

Like a hurricane survivor, Mrs. Bassett made her way through this confusion, going around after her husband, picking up, setting things right.

But now she'd be busy with her pups. Probably in bed for a couple of days, while Pete did the housework. What a prospect for a new mother, thought Shep, walking around to the back of the house. Moving a trash pail that was standing in the middle of the path, he mounted three kitchen steps and knocked.

Pete sprang at the door like a dog with a snake at his heels. He did not look the way Shep thought a brand-new first father should . . . happy and proud and benevolent. He looked hot and peevish and bewildered.

"Shep!" he exclaimed. "Oh, what a relief. Look—Bridget wants an omelet. Don't you think—considering everything—I mean *seven* of them—cute little devils, but doesn't seven seem sort of too—well—*much*?"

"It's quite a lot," Shep said cautiously.

"But don't you think—I mean, she's entitled to an omelet, right?"

"Anyone say she isn't?"

"No, but look . . . look . . ."

Groaning, Pete dragged the deputy toward a big iron range. "Look there at that mess, Shep. I mean, really take a *look* at—that's the third one I've tried to . . . I mean, I don't seem to know how to make—you can see—"

He gestured at a sinkful of crumpled eggshells.

"I can't afford this, Shep. I've got only a dozen laying hens and half of them are sulking for some reason—but she *wants* an

omelet. And at such a time . . . I mean, all those puppies, you never saw such a sight—"

His jowly face sagged further, his ears seemed to get longer, his eyes filled with tears of perplexity.

Shep gazed down at the skillet. In the middle of it lay a round, brown, shriveled thing, looking like a small cowpat.

"I can't serve her that, can I?" said Pete. "A brand-new mother—I mean, what sort of—" He broke off, looking ready to break down.

"*I* wouldn't," Shep said.

"You wouldn't *what?*" Pete yelped.

"Serve her that omelet."

"Oh. I didn't know what you—Shep, you're a bachelor. Bachelors are supposed to be good cooks, aren't—can you make an omelet?"

"I could do a better one than that."

"So, will you—will you? I've got three eggs left, that's all. I was trying to decide what to do after—I mean, there's no reason to think my fourth try would be any better than—do you want an *apron*? I've got another apron—I expect you'll want to wear a—"

Funny, thought Shep, I never noticed before that he doesn't even finish his sentences. How does he get anything done at all?

Tying the apron on, he instructed Pete to wash the skillet thoroughly, broke the three remaining eggs expertly into a clean bowl, and got to work.

Ten minutes later, on a tray was a puffy golden omelet folded over apricot preserves. From his garden, Pete had provided a tomato, slightly overripe, to slice, and a sprig of parsley, slightly wilted, for garnish. Two pieces of toast, a glass of milk, and they had a nice invalid tray.

Pete added, at the last minute, a yellow cosmos in a jelly jar.

"Just the right touch," Shep said approvingly.

"Then it's the first right touch I've managed all day."

"Oh now, Pete. Don't keep putting yourself down. You—" Shep stopped, looked around the kitchen for something to comment upon favorably, found nothing, and said heartily, "You're doing fine, Pete. Just fine."

"Thanks," said Pete in his sad rumble. "I appreciate that, Shep—really I do. I appreciate all your help in this—I don't know what I'd have—I know what! I'll write a letter of commendation about you to the paper. That's what I'll—"

"Don't!" said Deputy Shep in alarm. "I mean, making omelets isn't in the manual. Phil'd have my badge. Just take it that I've had a good time doing a good turn and let it go at that."

"If you *say* so, Shep, but after all you've done—"

"Believe me, I say so."

Bridget Bassett, the seven puppies sprawling about her, sat up with an expression of surprise and delight at their entrance. She did not look like an invalid, and Shep doubted if she'd be in bed another day. How could anybody lie comfortably upstairs knowing Pete was taking charge of things downstairs? Being married to him, Shep thought, must be like living in a house that's always catching on fire and springing leaks.

He admired the sevenfold litter as heartily as possible—not being one to dote on young ones, especially not day-old young ones—and explained that he had to get back on duty.

Just the same, he thought, pedaling

back to the main road, if I didn't do another thing tonight but make that omelet, and even if it was outside the line of duty and not in the regulations or the manual, I haven't wasted my time. No matter what Sheriff Phil English would say.

If he found out about it.

Which I sure hope he doesn't, Shep said to himself. Especially when I'm really supposed to be looking for Widow Colly's mare.

VI

As HE TURNED from the lane onto the main road, Deputy Shep saw Chief Dal race by and head toward the firehouse, brass bell raising a clangor, Henry's hooves raising a whirlwind of dust.

Shep lifted his nose and sniffed the air. One foot on the ground, he turned full circle, inspecting sky and countryside. No sign of fire that he could detect. No scorching reek, no drifting smoke. Nothing to indicate that Dal had been about his business of subduing a blaze.

Was Chief Dal just exercising himself, Henry, and the wagon? He'll have all the dogs this side of town out of bed, thought Shep. Indeed, lights were going on in houses here and there and awakened sleepers were rushing out in their nightclothes to see what was the matter.

"What is it? What's all the racket about—"

"Will somebody tell me what's going on out here?"

"Is there a fire, or isn't there? . . ."

"Who's in charge here? Does anybody know who's in charge?"

"If there's a fire, we have a right to know where—"

"Hey, Shep! You there, Deputy! Where's the fire?"

"Officer Shep! I demand an explanation of—"

"I believe," Shep said, "that Chief Dal

is making sure his equipment is in perfect condition. Which we want him to do, don't we?"

"Oh, indeed!" exclaimed Mrs. Aire-Setter, her nightcap askew. "Are we to be dragged terrified from our beds in this fashion because Chief Dal is inconsiderate, irresponsible, unthinking, ignorant of the hour and—"

"He's not irresponsible—" Shep began,

and was interrupted on all sides.

"I agree with Mrs. Aire-Setter," Klaus Dachs snapped. "Let this fellow see to his equipment by daylight is all I have to say. And furthermore—"

"It's a matter for the police," Mr. Aire-Setter shouted. "My wife is upset. I'm going to call a constable and lodge a complaint."

"That's the thing to do!" said his neighbor, a nervous terrier named Foxx. "Call the cops!"

"That's me," Deputy Shep pointed out. "I am the cops."

"So you are, so you are," Mr. Aire-Setter admitted. "Very well, Officer . . . I want you to swear out a warrant against Chief Dal."

"On what charge?"

"Disturbing the peace! Disturbing the peace!" Mr. Foxx yipped, dancing on clattery claws. "Scaring folk with his wheels and his bell and his great galloping horse."

Shep lifted a restraining paw. "I ask you all please to go back in your houses. Go to bed. I'll have a talk with the chief."

"A warrant!" said Mr. Aire-Setter. "I demand that there be a warrant—the fellow should be behind bars, that's what I say."

"Deputy Shep!" Major Ridgeback barked. "I fear I shall have to register a formal protest with your superior officer. Your conduct is not commendable. When I was on active duty this sort of thing—"

"Stop at the station house in the morning, Major. I'll be glad to take your complaint."

"I *said* I shall speak to your superior. I deal only with superiors."

"Tomorrow I will be my superior. It's my turn to turn sheriff."

"Oh." The major looked taken aback. "So it is. Well. Well, I'll overlook the matter this time. But you go and see Chief Dal immediately. Express our strong disapprov—"

"I'm going," Shep growled. He mounted his bicycle and pedaled off, leaving the crowd to mutter and disperse on its own.

At the firehouse a few minutes later, he found the chief singing as he sloshed and washed his fire wagon. Henry was clumping and chomping again in his stall. As Shep came in, he tossed his head and whinnied.

You'd think it was the middle of the day, Shep thought.

He sat on a stool and fiddled with some brass screws in a pail beside him. "Dal, do you realize you've got practically everyone this side of town out of bed?" he said at last.

"That so?" said the chief. "Nice night for it." He turned to the deputy with a dreamy smile. "Have you noticed how many fireflies there are of late, Shep? Winking their little lanterns all over the place. I'm glad I don't have to put *them* out, the little devils—"

He's babbling, thought Shep in alarm. He's gone gaga. "Listen, Dal—*they* don't think it's a nice night to be got out of bed in the middle of it—"

"Didn't know fireflies *had* beds, Shep."

"Dal! I think the major's going to have you court-martialed."

The fire dog sat beside Shep and got out his pipe. He smiled and said nothing.

"Look here, Chief. What are you doing racing around at this hour? There's no sign of a conflagration that I can see."

"I'll tell you, Shep. It's a simple, beautiful story that I am happy to relate, and you as my friend will be happy to hear. You see, Henry and I were out, making sure that the wagon and hose and water tank were all up to sniff. Henry was walking quietly and I wasn't even touching the bell, when I chanced to pass close to Madame Colette's—"

"Chanced."

"Passed close by, in any case. And there she was, rushing onto the porch in a frilly little gown—it had blue bows on it, Shep— or maybe they were little flowers, I was too preoccupied to make sure—"

"Get on with it, will you?"

"I was trying to give you a picture—"

"I want you to give me an explanation. The sheriff isn't going to like it if I can't give him a reason why you got the whole town in an uproar." He paused. "It's a good thing Phil lives at the other end of town, or you might be in the lockup this minute."

"And if there was a fire? What then?"

"Chief, I think Phil would take Henry and the wagon and try to put it out himself. There's nothing he thinks he can't do.

Now, will you *please* get on with your explanation, or I'll run you in myself."

Again Chief Dal gave him a dreamy look. "Madame Colette came tripping out of her door just as I passed by, her sweet face the picture of alarm, so naturally I reined Henry in and rushed to her side."

"And?" Shep prompted, when the chief again fell silent.

"Hmm? Oh. Ah—well, a small blaze had flared up in her drawing-room stove. You should see that room, Shep—white, with pink and blue chintz and the stove has flowers painted on it and there's the prettiest mirror over the—"

"Chief!"

"All *right*. I just thought you'd be inter—"

"What's she got a fire going for at this time of year?"

"She was trying to burn some boxes and one had fallen on the hearth rug. I soon

61

put things right. And then, do you know what?"

"Well, *what?*" Shep said after a pause.

"Shep—I can scarcely believe it yet! She let me hold her paw! Her dear little darling paw!"

Deputy Shep blinked. "You held her personal paw? No wonder bells were ringing. Of course once I explain that to everybody, they'll see that there was nothing you could do except get them all out of bed."

The fire chief sighed. "A sweet and generous reward for such trifling assistance. You can see how it's affected me."

"We all *heard* how it affected you. And I haven't heard you talk this much since kindergarten. You're making me nervous," the deputy said. He got out his notebook and wrote, *Ch. D. ext'd dr. rm. blze at res. of Mme. C. at*— Chief Dal extinguished drawing-room blaze at residence

of Madame Colette at— He glanced up. "At what time did you render this professional assistance?"

The chief didn't answer. He walked to the firehouse door and stood looking from one side of the horizon to the other.

"What a beautiful night," he said.

Shep got up. "Talking to you is a waste of breath," he said. "I'm going back to the station house and eat. It's way past my dinner hour."

"*Bon appetit.*"

"*What?*"

"French, Shep. It's French for enjoy your dinner. I'm thinking of learning the language, just in case—"

Deputy Jack Shep hopped on his bicycle and sped away. He couldn't look a moment longer at the silly lovestruck expression on his friend's face.

VII

So FAR AS Deputy Shep knew, Phil English never took a mid-tour-of-duty snooze.

"Every dog to his taste," Shep said to himself, stretching out on the bench beneath the window. "That's always been my motto." He was asleep in moments, Chief Dal, Widow Colly's mare, Mrs. Peke's ruby collar quite forgotten.

Waking an hour later, he flexed his muscles, clapped on his cap, and set forth on his second round of the town, now truly in darkness. No lights anywhere except for streetlamps and, far down the road, that of the firehouse. Church bells, stilled at midnight, would not ring again until six o'clock. There was not a footfall to be heard. Even the cats had gone off to wherever cats go when they disappear.

Strange creatures, cats, Shep mused, pedaling slowly, no hands. Unpredictable. Even Beanblossom. He wondered, as he pumped lazily through the village, what went on in the heads of cats, birds, goldfish, turtles—the pets that dogs kept for company.

He couldn't be sure, but supposed that nothing much occurred to a fish or a turtle in the course of a day. But your Siamese cat, he said to himself, or your pet raven (Major Ridgeback kept one of those), surely they had *some* opinions—about life, about food, about the dogs who presumed to "own" them.

He would never know what Beanblossom really thought about him. Nor would

Major Ridgeback know what Peppin was thinking as he sat on his perch watching all that went on.

And maybe that's just as well, he decided.

These reflections were interrupted by the sound of thudding hooves. Cantering toward him down the road came Ethelbert Peke, the Enoch Pekes' adolescent son, bareback on a bay horse, clutching the mane, swaying from side to side.

"Well, well, well," said the deputy to himself. "Can that horse I see before me be the vanishing Fancy That? Can it be that with so little effort I've found the missing mare that I've forgotten to look for?"

"Hey there, Bert!" he shouted. "What do you think *you're* up to?"

For a Pekingese, Ethelbert was a tough young customer, as anyone who called him anything but Bert was quick to find out. He had taken on dogs four times his size and forced them to say "Uncle," or—what came to the same thing—"Bert."

Deputy Shep was no admirer of young dogs, who seemed to him rowdy, raucous, rude, and disrespectful of gardens. Nevertheless, he liked Bert, who'd been hanging around the station house since his puppyhood, whenever he wasn't on a sandlot at the edge of town, throwing stones at tin cans, hitting maybe one in fifty but never giving up. Bert said he couldn't decide if he wanted to become a police dog or pitch for the Houndstown Hotdogs.

"Whoa there! Both of you!" Deputy Shep commanded, and raised an arresting paw. Bert tumbled off the mare and rolled laughing along a grassy stretch. The horse galloped on.

Deputy Shep pushed his cap back as he watched the flying hooves of the little bay mare. Even if he hadn't left the snaffle bit on the desk in the station house, there'd be no use trying to catch her.

Turning to young Peke, his eyes widened and he caught his breath in shock. Lying on the grass, a few inches from where Bert sprawled, was a bejeweled dog collar!

Oh, my goodness, Deputy Shep thought unhappily. This is terrible. This is absolutely awful. The perp is Peke's pup!

"Son," he said, "you have a lot of explaining to do. Why are you out at this time of night, what were you doing with the Widow Colly's horse?" He paused. "And—it's difficult for me to find words for what I am obliged to ask now—"

He broke off. Never—*never*—would he have dreamed that young Bert, this lad he'd known and cared about since he was a pup, could become a—

He would not say the word, even to himself.

"Oh, is that Mrs. Colly's horse?" Bert

asked, brushing himself off. "How was I to know? How do *you* know?"

"Since her bay mare is missing, and that's the only loose mare I've seen tonight, I think the question answers itself. Now—you answer me, Bert—though what you can say—"

Bert scratched his ear. "What I'm doing out at this hour—you want to know that? Well, it's like this. I got sent to bed without supper because of sassing Pop. I mean, he calls it sassing when I ask a question. I think I was only saying that if the dumb old collar is so valuable, why do they leave it lying around that way—"

"Yes. The collar. I am waiting for an explanation about the—"

"I don't like being locked in my room without supper," Bert interrupted. "So I climbed out the window and went out back to the barn. I keep a tin of cookies there,

71

in case of emergencies. And listen, Sheriff—"

As Bert called both policemen Sheriff, regardless of which one actually was, Shep ignored that and said roughly, "I am not interested in where you keep spare cookies. Explain *this*, if you can." He leaned over, picked up the collar, and shook it in the young dog's face. "I'm listening, Ethelbert."

"Hey! Don't call me that—"

"I'll call you whatever suits me. *Now!* What are you doing with your mother's jewelry that's been reported stolen?"

Looking unhappy, but not in the least guilty, Bert waved his tail from side to side in a considering manner, then sat on the grassy bank. "I suppose I have to tell you."

"You certainly do. I will not believe that you stole this thing, or the mare, no matter how things look, but I have to know what you were doing with the horse and what you're doing with this valuable ruby dog collar that belongs to your mother."

Bert Peke sighed. "It's this way, Sheriff . . . I was back in the barn, see, eating cookies, when this pretty little mare wandered in and starting helping herself to my father's coach horse's oats. So I let her eat for a bit, and then I thought what fun it would be—to ride her bareback. Not for long, you know. Just a little canter down the road . . ."

"Get to the point, Bert. What you were doing with the mare is now beside it. Unless you plan to be a horse thief, too."

"Sheriff, you know I didn't steal anything—"

"How come you have your mother's ruby collar?"

Bert studied the ground in silence, then got to his feet. "It's better if I show you. Can I ride on your handlebars?"

They bicycled back to the center of town

in silence, stopping in front of Enoch
Peke's solid, many-gabled house.

"Put your bike in the bushes there,"
Bert whispered, "and follow me round
back. You better take your bicycle lamp."

They made their way along the path beside the house, past extensive gardens. Bert
took the lamp from Deputy Shep and held
it high as they walked on tiptoe toward the

far end of the dark and lofty barn. In his stall, Enoch's coach horse moved restlessly. Up in the rafters, something fluttered and was still.

"Look there," whispered Bert, holding the bicycle lamp so its light fell in a corner where a tattered wicker sewing basket, past use, was crammed full of—full of what?

"What *is* all that junk?" Shep asked, gazing at a jumble of paper clips, pennies, hairpins, broken Christmas tree ornaments, children's jacks, a few dominoes, several of Chief Dal's brass screws—he couldn't count the number of useless objects that filled the basket.

But!

In with the junk were a cameo brooch, a beribboned war medal, a silver spoon, and a collection of buttons. Some of tarnished metal, some shiny and pearllike, some brightly colored.

"Buttons," muttered Jack Shep. "A

bunch of buttons. What do you know?"

"So you see, Sheriff," said Ethelbert Peke, "this is where I found Mother's ruby collar. And what do you say to that, huh?"

VIII

DEPUTY SHEP REMOVED his cap and sat down heavily on the barn floor. "Tell me, Bert. Do you know what this is all about?" He waved a paw at the sewing basket.

"I think so. You see, one night when I came out here to eat cookies—I can't remember why I was locked in my room that time, but anyway I was—I saw in front of me this little brown old rat running along with a spoon in his mouth. 'Well,' I said to myself, 'that's a peculiar sight.' "

He paused for questions, but the deputy said nothing.

"So I followed him, of course."

"Of course."

"He went right to this corner," the Peke pup continued eagerly. "Which was how I knew where to look for the ruby collar. I mean, I never did think it was stolen. Not *really* stolen. That first time I saw him, the rat, I mean, it wasn't quite dark, and I could see all right, but I hung back—not wanting to alarm him, you know—and by golly, he went to this basket and put the spoon on top of the rest of the junk. And then do you know what he did?"

"Took one of those buttons"—Shep indicated the collection—"and went off with it."

"How did you know?"

"I'm a cop. I deducted it. How did you know your mother's collar would be here? You deducted it. You've the makings of a detective yourself, Bert." And nosy enough to make sheriff easily.

"Really?" said the young Peke with pleasure. "Actually, I don't think I could ever hurl for the Hotdogs, do you?"

"I don't think you could pitch for the Chihuahua Little League."

"Yeah. I don't think so, too. So I'm going to be a police dog, just like you."

He'll be a better one than I am, thought Shep. Or Phil English, for that matter. I'm too lazy to be a good law officer. And Phil's so stuffed with the police manual that he can't think for himself. But young Bert here. Bursting with energy and curiosity and independence, is Bert. Just the stuff to make a fine police dog.

"So, to sum up," he said, "when you heard that your mother's valuable ruby dog collar was gone missing, you knew where to look for it."

"Sure thing."

Probably be *county* sheriff one day. Chief

of detectives. *Commissioner.*

"Why didn't you inform the law about this cache, once you'd found it?"

"Well, heck, Sheriff. I couldn't rat on such a nice rat, now could I? I mean, probably I would've told *you* someday. Maybe. But not Sheriff English. Heck, he'd lock him up. Only now, with my mother swooning around all day, I had to check and see if the collar was here, didn't I? And I've told you about it, haven't I? But he's a *nice* rat, and I don't want him arrested. I mean, do you have to—"

"Bert! Stop talking for one second, will you? I can't think with you rattling on like that."

"Okay." After a minute, the high young voice continued, "What do we do now?"

"*You* do nothing. It's my problem."

"Hey! Don't I have anything to say? I mean, I told you this in secret, and it isn't fair for you to—"

"Will you keep still and let me figure this out?"

"Yeah, but—"

"QUIET!" Shep barked, shocking Bert into silence.

Deputy Shep clapped on his cap. He thought he could think better with it on. He got up and began to pace, which he thought increased the flow of blood to his brain.

What a tour of duty this was proving to be. Stolen jewelry. Runaway horses. Furious citizens awakened from sleep by a lovesick fire dog. Blundering new fathers. Omelets!

And now this rat burglar to do something about. Had he said Canoville was a peaceful village?

"What are you going to *do*?" Bert persisted.

"I'm not sure yet," Shep snapped.

"When will you be?"

"Ethelbert! The law has been broken. That's a fact."

"I know, but—"

"But there are circumstances."

"What circumstances?"

"I believe we are dealing here with a pack rat," said Shep.

"A pack rat?"

"An interesting species. He can't help stealing shiny things. It's his nature. But he's not your everyday perp, because he tries to give as good as he takes."

"How does he go about doing that?"

"When a pack rat filches something, he leaves something in its place. This rat leaves buttons. I suppose, to his way of thinking, it's a fair exchange."

"He's only a little rat, right? How would he know the difference between a ruby collar and a button? I think he's being *very* fair."

Shep studied his young companion. Maybe not a future police dog at all. Lawyer for the defense?

Suddenly Bert pricked up his ears, doused the lantern, and whispered, "I think I hear him coming now. Let's get back in the shadows."

In moonlight streaming through the barn door they saw a small brown rat skim over straw-strewn boards, smooth as if on wheels. In his teeth was a yellow rubber mouse.

Turning his head from side to side, the rat approached the basket cautiously, then put the toy mouse on top of his pile of treasures.

"Isn't he *nice*?" Bert whispered. "I bet he's got children at home. I bet they're twins. I bet he doesn't lock them in their room. I bet—"

"Keep still while I watch him," said Shep.

Selecting and discarding a couple of buttons, the rat found one to his liking and scampered out of the barn with it.

Shep walked over and looked in the basket. "What do you know, Bert? He's hit *my* house. Look at those green glass eyes. That's Beanblossom's toy mouse. It has her teeth marks on it, and a red spot where I got ink on it."

Bert Peke burst out laughing, then said quickly, "Hey, but Sheriff, you won't run him in just because he burgled *you*, will you?"

"I wouldn't think of it. But Phil English would. Goes by the book, Phil does."

"Couldn't you just not tell him?"

"What about your mother's ruby collar? What do we do about that?"

"I've been studying that, Sheriff. What I think is this—I take the collar and pretend to find it. I'll say the cat knocked it off the mantel."

"You'd be lying. I won't be a party to that."

"Then you tell me—what *do* we do?"

"What *you're* going to do is give me the collar. You will then sneak back to your room and start behaving yourself. No more midnight rides on stray mares, no more climbing out of windows. If your father puts you in your room, stay there and starve. You probably deserve to."

"But hey, Sheriff—that's leaving me out of everything. It isn't fair."

"I hope you aren't trying to go through life expecting it to be fair."

"It could be *sometimes*. Like now."

"I suppose you're right. Tell you what, Bert—you come around to the station house tomorrow morning, and I'll give you a full report. Not written," he added hastily. "An oral report."

Deputy Shep collected the cameo brooch, the silver spoon, the war medal, and Beanblossom's mouse. He poked around to see if there was something else *v.v.val*. He couldn't see that there was.

He and Bert walked out of the barn, and Shep watched until the young Peke had climbed up the trellis and in through the open window of his bedroom.

Back at the station house, he looked at the clock. Three hours before Sheriff English was due. Never until tonight had a tour of duty seemed so long. He wished Bert had never showed him the pack perp's secret hoard. He wished he had not become a cop.

He put the yellow mouse in his pocket, dropped the collar, the cameo, the spoon, and the medal on the desk. How was he to get the things back to their owners without explanation either to them or to the sheriff?

"I always knew I should've been a gardener," he muttered, and glanced up as a huge shadow loomed at the door.

Doctor Dane tramped in, sank to a chair, and sighed. "Any coffee around here, Shep?"

"Sure thing, Doc. You had to get up again, eh?"

"I did. Mrs. Aire-Setter was having a nervous turn—something about fire alarms, I didn't listen carefully. Her husband came around and woke me up asking for something to put her to sleep. Thanks," he said, accepting the mug Shep handed him. He glanced at the desk. "Is that a ruby collar I see before me?"

"It is."

"Mavis Peke's?"

"Yup."

"And those other things?"

"Mrs. Whippet's cameo, Mrs. Aire-Setter's spoon, and Major Ridgeback's war medal."

"You've solved the case? Congratulations."

"It's not that easy, Doc." Deputy Shep sighed, frowned, and began, "See, the way it turned out—"

At the end of Shep's explanation, the doctor said, "I don't think it's such a terrible problem. I pass Enoch's on my way home. And I can go a bit out of my way to the Major's and Mrs. Whippet's and the Aire-Setters'. I'll drop the things in their mailboxes. That way you won't have to explain to anyone. Besides, it'll be a nice little mystery for the town to gnaw on. Do everybody good."

"You think we can get away with it?"

"Of course," said the big doctor, getting to his feet. "Thank you for letting me in on the doings, Shep. It's quite refreshed me."

After he'd gone, taking the stolen property with him, Deputy Shep got out his notebook, studied it a moment, tore up the notes he'd made, and dropped the pieces in the trash can.

Pulling the blotter toward him, he wrote, *A.q. Nthng to rpt.* All quiet. Nothing to report.

Presently Sheriff English would turn up and turn into Deputy English, thereby turning Shep into Sheriff.

He wasn't worried. After all that had gone on tonight, he didn't think there'd be another crime wave in Canoville for at least six months.

He yawned. Time for a little snooze before he went home to feed Beanblossom and give her back her yellow mouse.

About the Author

MARY STOLZ is the distinguished and versatile author of dozens of books that are perennial favorites of young readers. Several of her books, including A WONDERFUL, TERRIBLE TIME; A DOG ON BARKHAM STREET; THE NOONDAY FRIENDS; and CAT IN THE MIRROR, have been chosen as ALA Notable Children's Books, and she is also the recipient of the George G. Stone Center for Children's Books 1982 Recognition of Merit Award honoring the entire body of her work. Among her most recent books for HarperCollins are the popular CAT WALK, THE EXPLORER OF BARKHAM STREET, THE SCARECROWS AND THEIR CHILD, STORM IN THE NIGHT, and GO FISH.

Born in Boston and educated at the Birch Wathen School and Columbia University in New York City, Mary Stolz now lives with her husband, Dr. Thomas C. Jaleski, on the Gulf Coast of Florida.

About the Illustrator

PAMELA JOHNSON has illustrated more than two dozen books for children, including four other books by Mary Stolz: CUCKOO CLOCK, PANGUR BAN, QUENTIN CORN, and TALES AT THE MOUSEHOLE.

She lives in Maine.